Children's Books:
Julia Loves Dolls

Sally Huss

Julia Loves Dolls

ISBN: 0692365133
ISBN 13: 9780692365137

Julia had a house full of dolls.

She had dolls that covered the walls

And dolls down both sides of the halls.

She had dolls on the refrigerator

And dolls on the air-conditioner.

There were dolls on the stairs…

And dolls in the chairs.

There were dolls in every closet in every room

And even a doll made out of the bristles of a broom.

There was hardly a place

In which you could not find a doll's face.

And every time Julia would open the door

Someone would show up with more.

At Christmastime Auntie Sue

Would send one or two.

And Uncle Ralph

Would add another to the house.

At Eastertime the Easter Bunny

Thought leaving one on her doorstep would be funny.

On Valentine's, more sweet dolls were added to the lines.

More dolls on President's Day

And more dolls on Earth Day!

There were so many dolls in Julia's house

There wasn't even room for one little mouse.

Julia's parents began to complain.

Her father yelled, "I can't see the TV to watch the game!"

And her mother began to fuss and fume

When she found dolls sitting on her bottles of perfume.

"Enough, Julia!" they began to scold.

"You can't have any more dolls than you can hold!"

"Oh my, my" fretted Julia, as she filled her arms to the brim.

This didn't even put a dent in the number of them.

That night as she went to sleep on the floor,

There wasn't any room on her bed anymore,

She thought about all the dolls that she had

And she thought about all the dolls that were sad.

Because a doll is meant to be played with and loved

And her dolls were stashed away, stored and shoved.

They were crammed into nooks and crannies,

From baby dolls to Barbies to Cabbage Patches to grannies.

They were covered with dust from lack of use…

"Oh, my gosh!" thought Julia, "This is doll abuse!"

"I will find arms to hold them and make them smile.

With all of these dolls, it might take awhile.

And I will keep only what I can love and take care of…

What I can play with and comb the hair of.

And I will give the rest away."

And that's what she began to do the very next day.

She found children's hospital wards that welcomed her dolls.

And church groups that collected dolls in the malls.

And at school, counselors found homes for each doll

Where there had not been a doll at all.

After two weeks of giving dolls away

Julia decided, "Now it's my turn to play."

But where were her dolls? She couldn't find them at all.

She looked in the closets and on the walls in the hall.

No dolls on the stairs.

No dolls in the chairs.

"Look outside. Look outside!"

Said her mother and father with pride.

"You've probably forgotten that it's your birthday today

With all of this giving of dolls away."

Out in the backyard under a tree

Was a dollhouse as pretty as it could be.

Julia's name was painted above the door

But inside there was even more in store…

A tea party with all of her favorite dolls seated here and there

And plenty of cake and cookies to share.

Then Julia said with a smile, as she sat down to tea,

"This is just the right number of dolls for me!"

So if you have a doll that is lacking your attention and care

Be sure to find another child with whom you can share.

A doll is to be loved and cuddled and never forgotten

No matter if it is made of porcelain, plastic, or cotton!

The end,
but not the end
of sharing.

At the end of this book you will find a Certificate of Merit that may be issued to any child who promises to honor the requirements stated in the Certificate. This fine Certificate will easily fit into a 5"x7" frame, and happily suit any girl or boy who receives it!

Here is another adorable, rhyming book by Sally Huss.

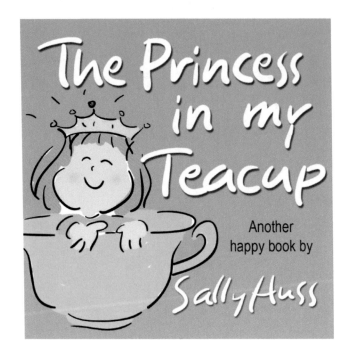

Description: What little girl would not want a princess to visit her? That's what kept happening to the little girl in this story. A princess would show up in a mud puddle, the kitchen sink, a bathtub, and even in a cup of tea. But it is what the princess told her that was most important, and the little girl took it to heart. Who was that princess in her teacup? You'll have to read the book to find out.

All in rhyme and accompanied by over 35 delightfully colorful illustrations that dance along with the story.

To learn more about THE PRINCESS IN MY TEACUP, you may go to: http://amzn.com/B00NG4EDH8.

If you liked JULIA LOVES DOLLS, please be kind enough to post a short review on Amazon by using this URL: http://amzn.com/B00LGYPHXE.

You may wish to join our Family of Friends to receive information about upcoming FREE e-book promotions and download a free poster – The Importance Happiness on Sally's website -- http://www.sallyhuss.com. Thank You.

More Sally Huss books may be viewed on the Author's Profile on Amazon. Here is that URL: http://amzn.to/VpR7B8.

About the Author/Illustrator

Sally Huss

"Bright and happy," "light and whimsical" have been the catch phrases attached to the writings and art of Sally Huss for over 30 years. Sweet images dance across all of Sally's creations, whether in the form of children's books, paintings, wallpaper, ceramics, baby bibs, purses, clothing, or her King Features syndicated newspaper panel "Happy Musings."

Sally creates children's books to uplift the lives of children and hopes you will join her in this effort by helping spread her happy messages.

Sally is a graduate of USC with a degree in Fine Art and through the years has had 26 of her own licensed art galleries throughout the world.

This certificate may be cut out, framed, and presented to any child who promises to honor the requirements stated here.

Certificate of Merit

(Name)

The child named above is awarded this Certificate of Merit for:

*Learning to share with others
*Practicing kindness
*Being friendly
*Learning to be helpful

Date: _____

Presented by: _____

Made in the USA
San Bernardino, CA
15 December 2015